Let us read to you!

Enjoy our complementary,
companion audiobook of

52

A TALE OF LONELINESS

as read by Patton Oswalt
by visiting umbrellybooks.com/52

52
A Tale of Loneliness

Written by
JOHNNY DePALMA

Illustrated by
KYLE BROWN

with Companion Audiobook
as read by PATTON OSWALT

UMBRELLY BOOKS

Umbrelly Books Publishing
Est. 2006, Campbell, CA

52 A TALE OF LONELINESS

For information regarding permissions, please contact:
Umbrelly Books Publishing

Additional Artwork by
Harmony Cornwell, Elan' Trinidad & Magnetic Dreams, Inc.
The Umbrelly Books logo, illustrated by Molly Crabapple
Edited by Robin Schroffel & Jennifer Wagner

Special thanks to

35, Nicholas, Diana Sotelo, Alexander, Demetri, Brileigh Brown, Cordelia Brown, Matt Abbott, Erica Arvold, Taylor Barron, Jeremy S. Bloom, Amanda Brown, Jim Callner, Gerald Carter, Larry Carothers, Will Chason, Moonlight & Chocolate, Olivia Cole, Kimberley Cranfield, Stephen Evans, Sam Fickinger, Kizzume Fowler, Deedra Garcia, Geneviève Godbout, Tyler Goll, Janelle Graves, Mike Halsey, Tracie Hart, Johnny Heller, Travis Howe, Kateryna Kosheleva, Madison Landis, Michael Lapinski, M. David Lee III, Margaux Lienard, Ashley Rae Little, Ashley Lovell, Tunuviel Luv, Vitaly Lyn, Ashley Malone, Savanah Martin, Abdel Pizarro, Chris Rodgers, Randall Saba, Eileen Siebken, Jennifer Torrey, William Watkins, Nathaniel Wolkstein, & Reeve Woolpert

For more information about this book, please visit our website www.umbrellybooks.com

First Edition
Manufactured in China
ISBN: 978-1-7334055-0-8

For Annie

**INSPIRED BY THE TRUE STORY
OF THE 52 HZ WHALE**

The ocean is a beautiful thing, my friend,
from shore to shore, and end to end.

Where peace, and rage, and cold attend.
The ocean is a beautiful thing.

And deep within its bellied ground,
invisible to all around,
there swims a whale named 52,
whose voice was sadly born askew.

"Hello, friends," he would start to say,
"not that you hear me anyway.

I know I'm not your average whale,
though I have the body, and the tail,

and yes, I swim from shore to shore
but sadly, still,

I think there's more.

Perhaps, it's just that... never mind.
It's not that other whales aren't kind.

They are, in fact! I know it's so! Where one will swim, the others go.
They talk, and sing, and joke about, and never fight, or scream, or shout.

They're just like me, except one thing, they can't quite seem to hear me sing.
Or talk, or joke, or swim, or be! I'm simply here, but they can't see.

For whales find whales not just with eyes, but also with their vocal cries.
Yet, ever since I've tried to call, it's like I'm not quite here at all.

But have no fear! I'm doing fine. I've found some ways to pass the time.
Ummm, lonely? Yes, but that's OK. I'm sure I'll have a friend someday.

And maybe they'll be just like you! Someone who's kind, and smart, and true.
That someone who will be a friend to those who need one in the end.

Still... I am quite happy most the time. It's not just me to which they're blind.
This ocean here that we call home, there's more to see when you're alone.

Like that! The sunlight trickles down on bubbles rising from the ground.
Or here! The way the water swirled. There's so much beauty in this world!

The little fish, they swim along. The whales, they sing their happy song.
The dolphins play, the seaweed grows,

the shark it comes, the shark it goes.

And that's all mine! I get to see
the things invisible, like me!

So every night, I say hello,
to all the barnacles below.

To every bubble, kelp, and shell. To every grain of sand as well.
For all these things make up my home, and with them,

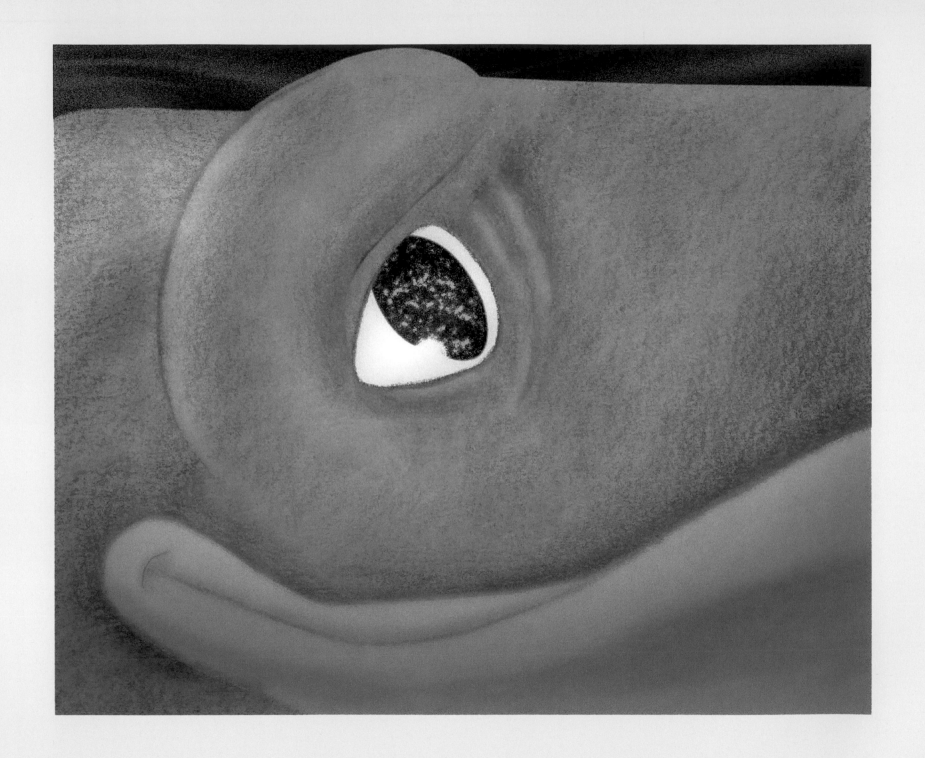

I don't feel alone.

Perhaps one day, they'll see it too,

instead of just this 'blur of blue.'

The magic swirling in the sea,

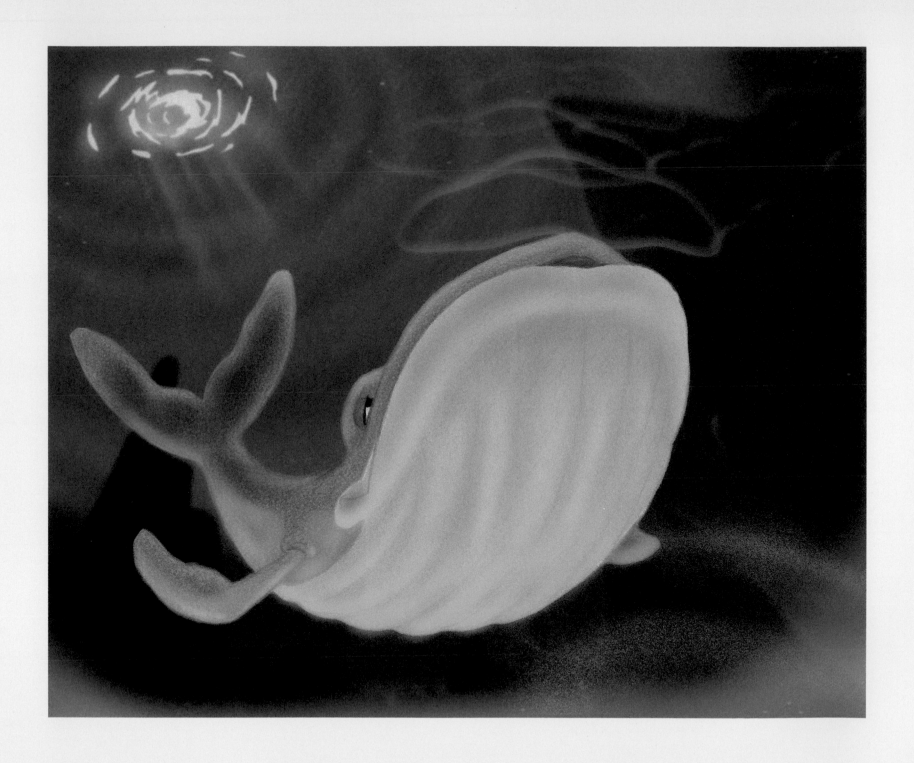

the whale that's calling out from me.

Sometimes I wish I were like them,

just playing games with all my friends.

We'd stay together all day long,

I'd find my voice, and sing my song.

But then,

I suppose I wouldn't be

the whale I am, and I like me!

It's true I'm happy,

and yet blue."

This lonely whale, named 52.

KYLE BROWN

Having started off as a self-taught graphic designer just outside of high school, Kyle Brown found his true calling in 2015 after illustrating his first children's book for Umbrelly Books Publishing entitled, *The Night Parade*. When he isn't illustrating, Mr. Brown enjoys writing, playing music, and raising a ruckus with his two incredible children around the Pacific Northwest. *52 – A Tale of Loneliness* is his third book.

JOHNNY DePALMA

In 2006, Johnny DePalma founded Umbrelly Books Publishing where he continues to grow his personal vision of unique children's literature. To date, Mr. DePalma has released six books, created one popular, albeit bizarre holiday, and brought home first place from the Bay Area Olympiad of Arts. Recently, he conceived and curated the Emergency Art Museum in his hometown of Campbell, CA. For more information, visit johnnydepalma.com

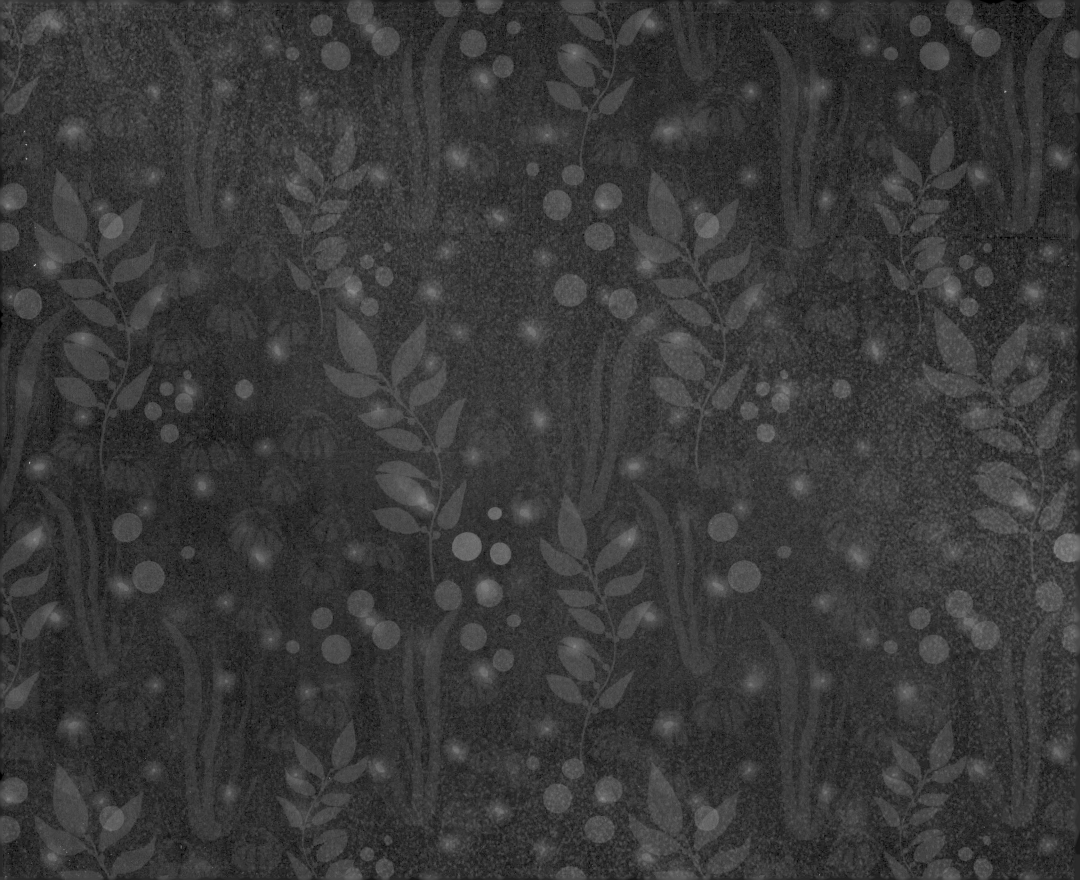